# OPEN VERY CAREFULLY

For Dylan, Sam and Alex
N.B.
For my Mum and Dad, who have always supported me
while letting me think I was doing it all by myself.
N.O.

# OPEN VERY

First published in 2013 by Nosy Crow Ltd
The Crow's Nest, 14 Baden Place
Crosby Row, London SE1 1YW
www.nosycrow.com

This edition published 2018 for Scottish Book Trust.

ISBN 978 1 78800 344 5

Nosy Crow and associated logos are trademarks
and /or registered trademarks of Nosy Crow Ltd.

Text Copyright © Nosy Crow 2013
Illustrations copyright © Nicola O'Byrne 2013

The right of Nicola O'Byrne to be identified as the
illustrator of this work has been asserted.

A CIP catalogue record for this book is available from the British Library.

Printed in China

1 3 5 7 9 8 6 4 2

# The Ugly Duckling CAREFULLY

Hans Christian Andersen

# Nicola O'Byrne

## With words by Nick Bromley

nosy
crow

**O**nce upon a time, there was a mother duck with three pretty ducklings and one . . .

Wait a minute!

What's that?

I'm trying to read you the story of The Ugly Duckling, but there's something in this book that shouldn't be here!

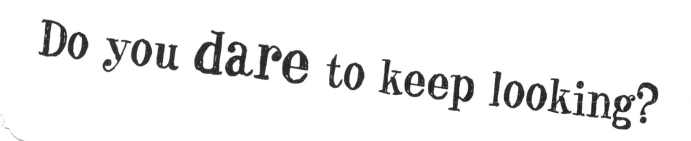

Do you **dare** to keep looking?

You do?

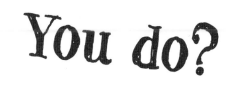

Then let's turn the page **very, very carefully...**

It's a ...

# ...CROCODILE!

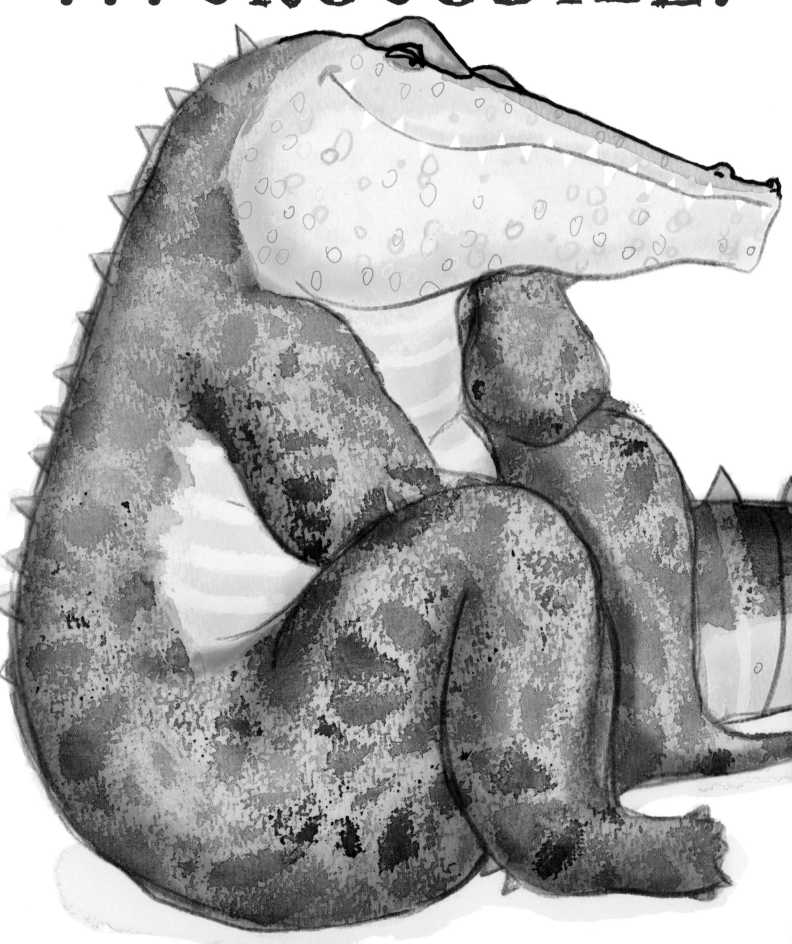

# A really big scary one!

What's he doing in
this book?

He might **bite** your finger.
Or **scratch** your nose!

I've heard crocodiles
like to do that.
Stay back
just in case . . .

# Watch out!
He's on the move.

What is he
doing?

He's eating
the letters!

He must be
hungry!

I think his favourite letters to eat are **O** and **S**.

**St p!**

**Mr Cr c dile!**

**Y u can't eat the letter !**

# Now he's gobbling up . . .

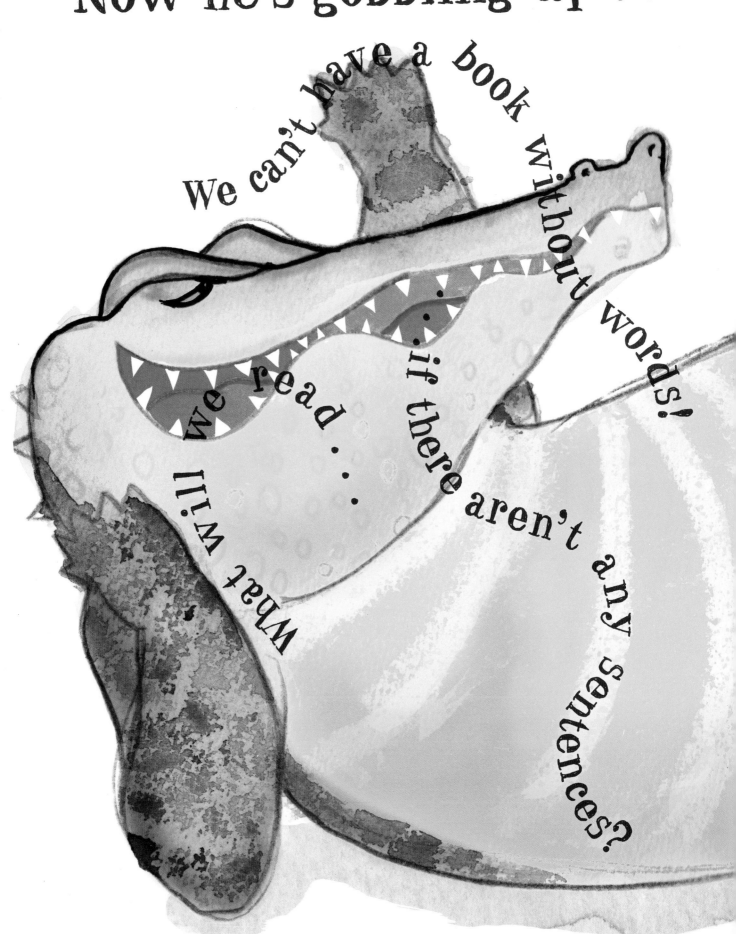

We can't have a book without words!

if there aren't any sentences?

We read . . .

What will

# ...whole words
## and
# sentences!

We've got to make him stop...

Let's try
rocking
the book

**backwards**

and

 **forwards.**

That's it . . .

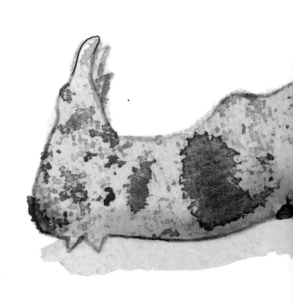

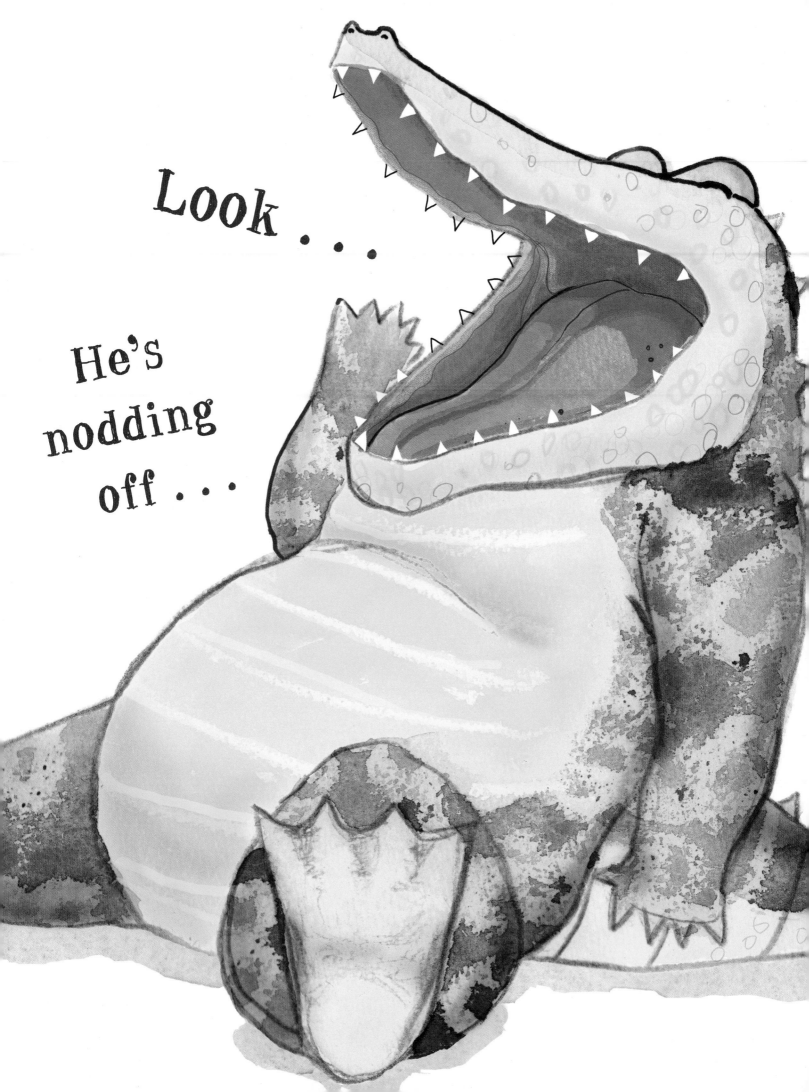

A A AHH . . .

He's sleeping like a baby.

I know . . .

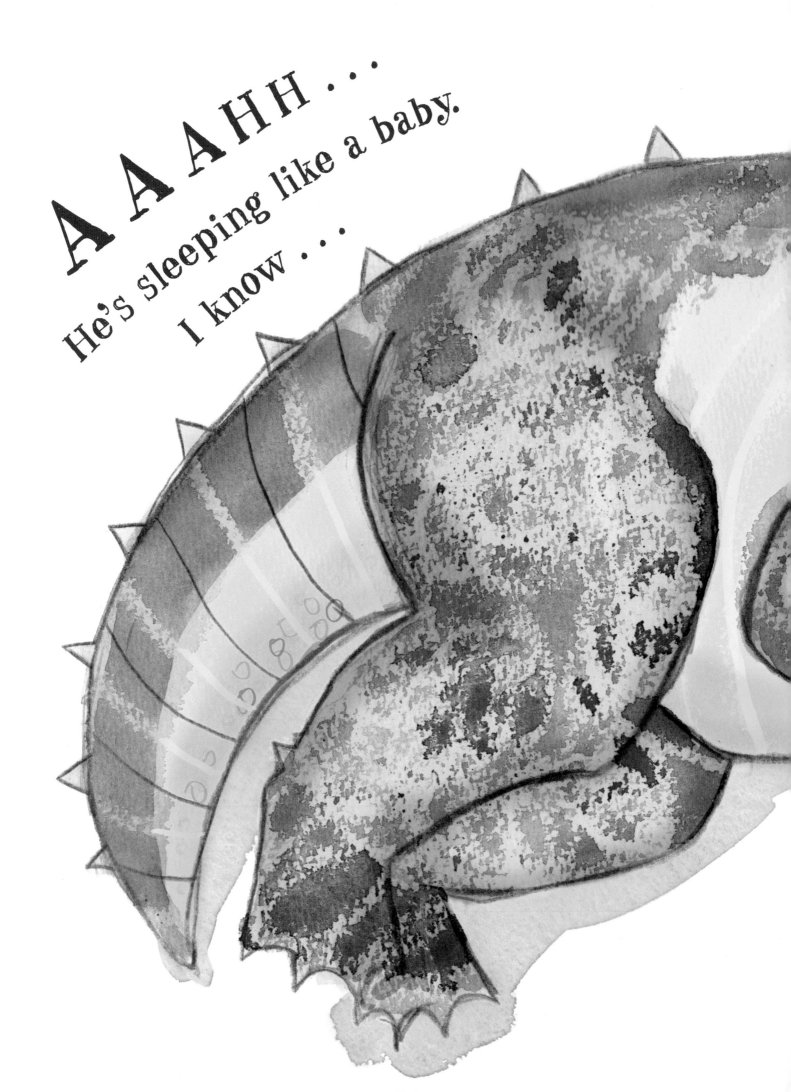

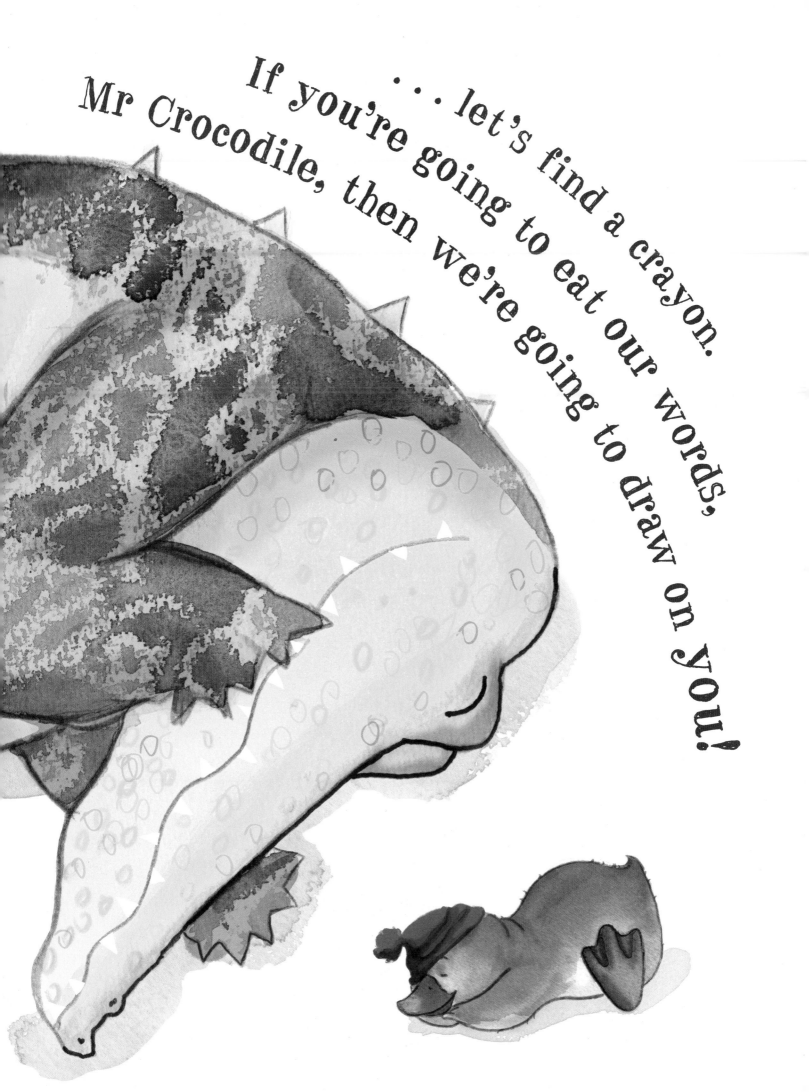

. . . let's find a crayon. If you're going to eat our words, then we're going to draw on you! Mr Crocodile,

SSSHHH...

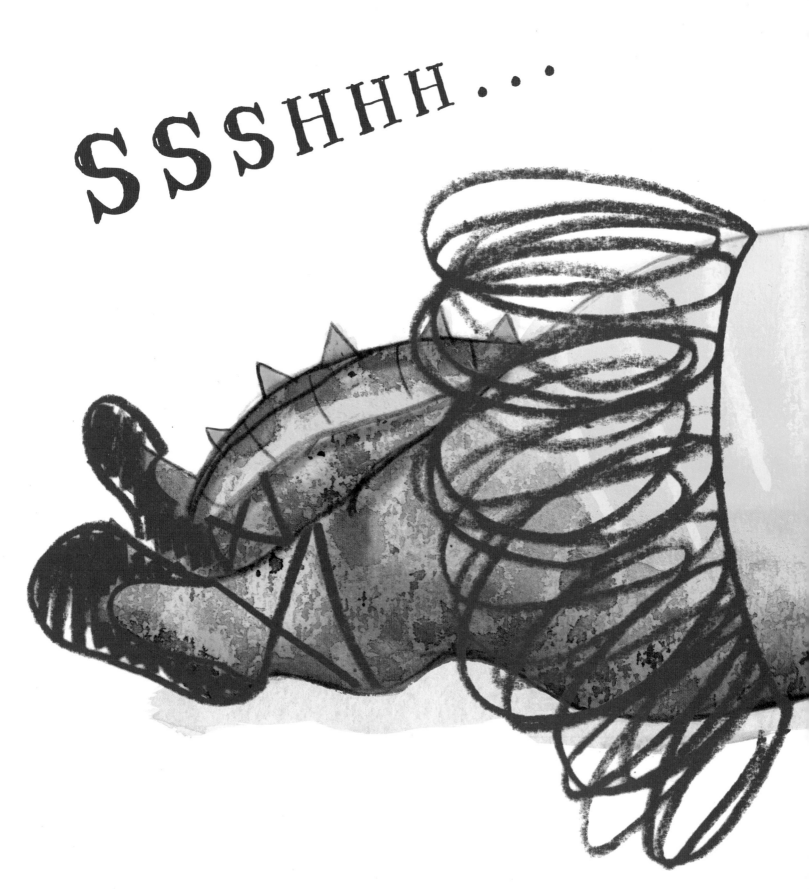

He's not such a scary

crocodile now!

Oh no!

Maybe he **is** a
**scary crocodile** after all!
All that drawing has
**woken him up!**

And he's not looking too happy
about that tutu.
Crocodiles **don't** do ballet!

# Watch out!

It looks as if he's had enough of this book . . .

I think he's going to make a run for it!

Here
he
goes . . .

# Ouch!

Well, who would
have thought it was so hard
to get out of a book?

Maybe if you
**shake**
the book,
he'll
fall
out.

Hmm. That didn't work either.

But look!

He's worked out
what to do.

He's munching a hole through the page.

And he is nearly out!

Goodbye, Mr Crocodile!

I wasn't scared.
Were you?